W9-BNG-280

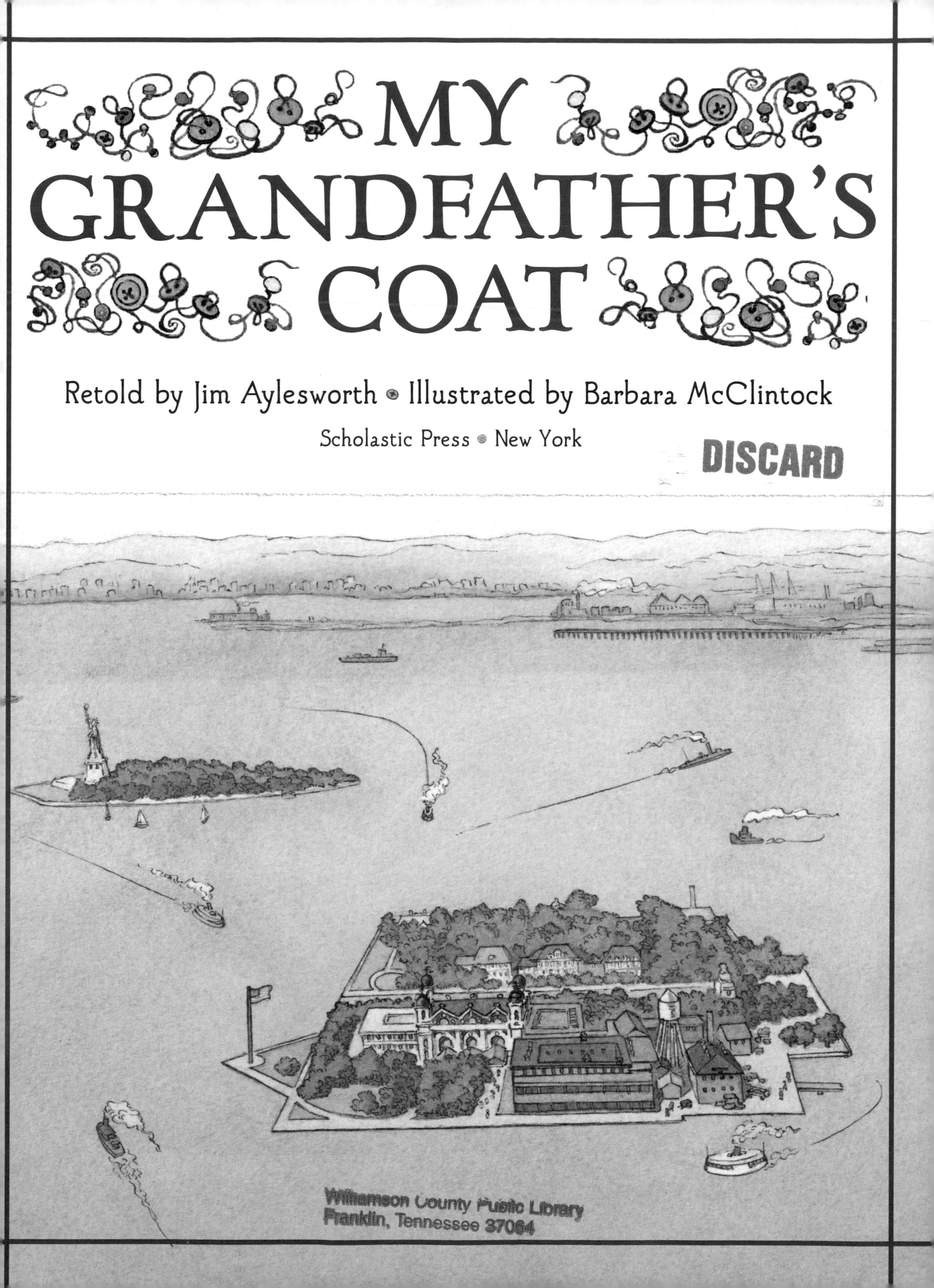

MY GRANDFATHER'S COAT

Retold by Jim Aylesworth • Illustrated by Barbara McClintock

Scholastic Press • New York

My grandfather came to America when he was very young. He came alone and with little more than nothing at all.

The years passed, and he became a tailor. He worked very hard.

And then, on the luckiest day of his life,
he met my grandmother, and they fell in love.

When she agreed to marry him, my grandfather went right to work.

He snipped, and he clipped,

and he stitched, and he sewed,

and he made for himself a handsome coat . . .

. . . that he wore on his wedding day!

My grandfather loved the coat,

and he wore it, and he wore it.

And little bit by little bit,

he frayed it, and he tore it,

until at last . . .

. . . he wore it out!

So what did my grandfather do?

He went right to work,

and he snipped, and he clipped,
and he stitched, and he sewed,

and out of the still-good cloth
of his handsome coat, he made . . .

. . . a smart jacket!

My grandfather loved the jacket,

and he wore it, and he wore it.

And little bit by little bit,
he frayed it, and he tore it,

until at last . . .

. . . he wore it out!

So what did my grandfather do?

He went right to work,

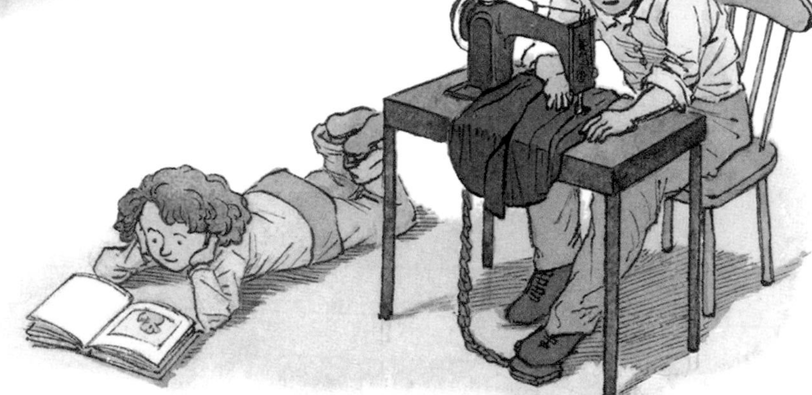

and he snipped, and he clipped,
and he stitched, and he sewed,

and out of the still-good cloth
of his smart jacket, he made . . .

. . . a snazzy vest!

My grandfather loved the vest,

and he wore it, and he wore it.

And little bit by little bit,
he frayed it, and he tore it,

until at last . . .

. . . he wore it out!

So what did my grandfather do?

He went right to work,

and he snipped, and he clipped,
and he stitched, and he sewed,

and out of the still-good cloth
of his snazzy vest, he made . . .

. . . a stylish tie that he wore on my mother's wedding day!

My grandfather loved the tie,

and he wore it, and he wore it.

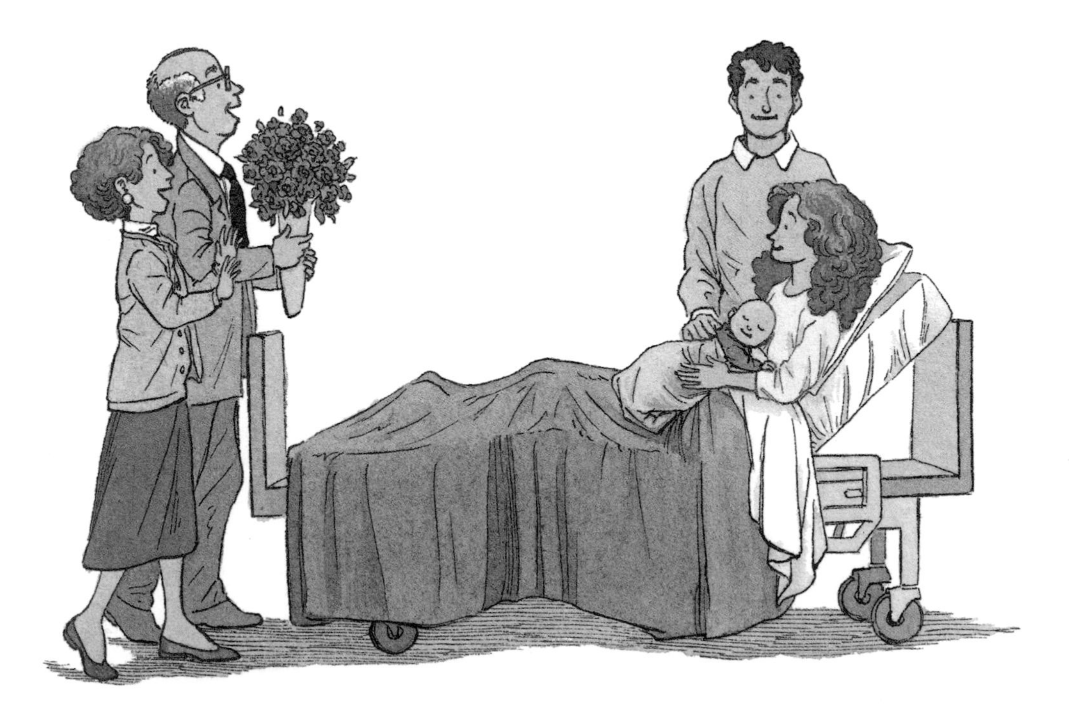

And little bit
by little bit,

he frayed it, and he tore it,

until at last . . .

. . . he wore it out!

So what did my grandfather do?

He sat right down,

and he snipped, and he clipped,
and he stitched, and he sewed,

and out of the still-good cloth of his stylish tie . . .

. . . he made a toy for you and your kittens!

You and the kittens loved the toy,

and you played with it,
and you played with it.

And little bit by little bit,
you tore it, and you frayed it,

until at last . . . you wore it out!

"It's okay," said my grandfather.
"*Nothing* has been wasted."

And up the stairs to bed
my grandfather carried you.

While tattered and torn, what little remained
of your kittens' toy was left lying on the floor.

And late, late, late,
when we were all soundly sleeping,

a mother mouse came creeping, creeping, creeping.
And she found it there.

Just the thing to make a nest!
thought the mother mouse.
And she pulled it across the floor.

And there, in her little house behind the walls,
she tore the threads apart,

and she puffed them,
and she fluffed them,

and out of those last bits of tattered cloth . . .

. . . she made a cozy nest!

There, she raised her family.

Then slowly, the threads moldered away
and moldered away . . .

. . . until there was nothing left at all.

No, nothing left of the cozy nest,

and nothing left of the kittens' toy,

and nothing left of the stylish tie,

and nothing left of the snazzy vest,

and nothing left of the smart jacket,

and nothing left at all of your
great-grandfather's handsome coat –

no, there was nothing left at all.

Nothing, that is, except for this story.

To all of those who came to America with so very little
and who did so very much to make our nation great!

– J. A.

With thanks to Ellen Graber Donohue and her family.
And to the early Jewish farm families who settled in rural America.

– B. M.

AUTHOR'S NOTE

My Grandfather's Coat is a retold story based on the beloved Yiddish folksong "I Had a Little Overcoat" (*"Hob Ikh Mir a Mantl"*). And much like the grandfather in this new version, this story motif also emigrated from its origins in eastern Europe to make a new life in America.

My ancestor the emigrant Aylesworth came in the mid-seventeenth century from England and settled in what is now Rhode Island, near modern-day Providence. So I am an eleventh-generation American, which is sort of rare. But my father-in-law did come through Ellis Island from Sicily as a child . . . like millions of Americans. And like the immigrants who came to America from everywhere in the world, they typically brought with them the attributes of hard work, thrift, and conservation, which served them well as they built their new lives here. I hope this story inspires you to create new things from what you have that are still good. And that it also inspires you to save those wonderful stories your families have to tell. And be sure to keep them in a safe place so you can share them with *your* children!

ARTIST'S NOTE

My great-grandparents passed through Ellis Island on their way from Norway to homestead farmland in North Dakota. I have fond memories of growing up there among the farm families who worked hard and were resourceful and thrifty.

I now live in northeastern Connecticut, where I set this book. I drew from my own family past. And, through local research, I discovered there had been an immigration program around the early part of the 20th century. It funded Jewish families from eastern Europe to leave the impoverished and crowded conditions of New York City to live and work on farms and in small American towns. Many came to this part of Connecticut. Tailors, grocers, teachers, doctors, lawyers, and store owners were also farmers. Farming was a way of life, and a poor tailor could grow produce, raise chickens, and sell eggs to feed his family and supplement the family income.

The synagogue in Hebron, Connecticut, which I used as a model for the wedding scene, was built in the 1940s. I love that this story, with Jewish roots, has now been retooled and transplanted onto American soil to be passed along to a new generation of readers.

The artist gratefully acknowledges the Jewish Historical Society of Greater Hartford, Connecticut; the United Brethren of Hebron Synagogue in Hebron, Connecticut; and the Lebanon Historical Society in Lebanon, Connecticut.

 Published by Scholastic Press, an imprint of Scholastic Inc., *Publishers since 1920.* • SCHOLASTIC, SCHOLASTIC PRESS, and associated logos are trademarks and/or registered trademarks of Scholastic Inc. • • Library of Congress Cataloging-in-Publication Data Aylesworth, Jim. • My grandfather's coat / retold by Jim Aylesworth ; illustrated by Barbara McClintock. – 1st ed. • p. cm. • Summary: A tailor's very old overcoat is recycled numerous times over the years into a variety of garments and other uses. • ISBN 978-0-439-92545-7 (hardcover : alk. paper) [1. Folklore – Europe, Eastern. 2. Coats – Folklore.] I. McClintock, Barbara, ill. II. Title. • PZ8.1.A887My 2012 398.2–dc23 [E] 2011012226 • 10 9 8 7 6 5 4 3 2 1 14 15 16 17 18 • Printed in Malaysia 108 • First edition, November 2014 • The display type was set in Forum Titling. • The text was set in Aged Book. • Barbara used a Hunt #100 steel pen nib and dip pen, Higgins Waterproof Ink, and Winsor & Newton Water Colours on Arches 90-pound cold press watercolor paper. • Book design by Chelsea C. Donaldson